Shitty M Gitty

AND

Cumbria
County Council

Libraries, books and more..........

Please return/renew this item by the last date shown.
Library items may also be renewed by phone on
030 33 33 1234 (24hours) or via our website

www.cumbria.gov.uk/libraries

Cumbria Libraries
CLIC
Interactive Catalogue

Ask for a CLIC password

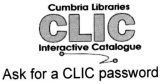

First published in the UK in 2017 by Nosy Crow Ltd
The Crow's Nest, 10a Lant Street
London, SE1 1QR, UK

Nosy Crow and associated logos are trademarks and/or registered
trademarks of Nosy Crow Ltd

1 3 5 7 9 10 8 6 4 2

A CIP catalogue record for this book will be available from the British Library.

Printed in Spain

Papers used by Nosy Crow are made from wood grown in
sustainable forests.

ISBN: 978 0 85763 848 9

www.nosycrow.com

CONTENTS

For Margaret,
with love...
T.C. x

To Valerie
and David.
S.L. x

Shifty McGifty and Slippery Sam

don't just make AMAZING cakes. These two brave bakers solve wacky mysteries too! Trouble might be just around the corner but Shifty and Sam are always ready…

Up, Up and Away!

Beep! Beep!

It was Rocky Road Race Day and Shifty and Sam were READY!

Their Bakemobile was gleaming. The boys were in their race suits. And their engine purred happily – prruuuum!

Peregrine Pug raised his megaphone. "All racers to the start line!" he called.

"Ooooo!" Sam wolfed down one last "lucky"

doughnut. "Let's go!"

As Shifty drove, Sam checked the race map. First they had to find their way through a corn maze, then race through Christmas Wood. After that, they'd head up Rocky Road Mountain, then down the other side to the finish line. Race Day was so exciting. They might even win the sparkly gold cup!

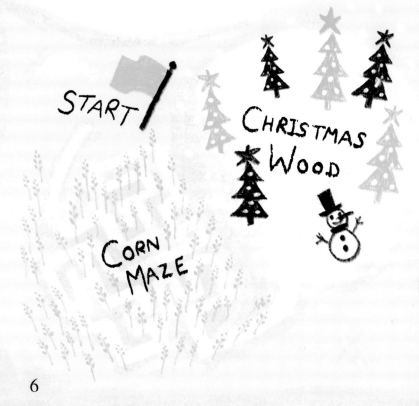

START

CHRISTMAS WOOD

CORN MAZE

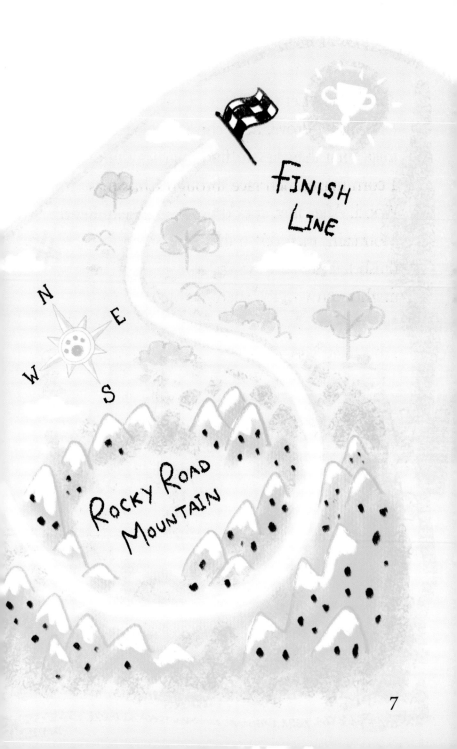

FINISH LINE

N
E
W
S

ROCKY ROAD MOUNTAIN

As the racers took their places at the start line, the boys saw some of their café customers. Duchess was racing her shiny limousine. Rover sat tall in his farm truck. And Matilda was in a double-decker bus with all of her fifteen puppies!

Then Fred pulled up in his vintage car. And there was Hercules on his sky-blue scooter.

FINISH LINE!

MAT 15

Hercules had never won a thing in his life, but that never stopped him trying. As Peregrine Pug was about to wave the start flag, one last-minute racer roared up. His jet-black car was as shiny as a crow, and looked like a cross between a castle and a tank.

"Eeek!" gulped Sam.

Then the boys spied the driver smirking down from his lookout tower. "Oh no!" Shifty tutted. And Sam rolled his eyes...

"Red Rocket!"

At the mention of his name the red panda puffed out his chest importantly, unaware that this just made him look like a teddy bear!

"Hello Doughnut-tum!" he said to Sam.
"And hello Giraffe-neck!" he said to Shifty.
Shifty and Sam shook their heads. They
would rather eat worms than race against their
annoying next-door neighbour.

For one thing, Red Rocket cheated. At everything. ALL the time.

And his silly old boasting drove everyone bananas!

Red Rocket looked them up and down. "My castle-car's better than your Bakemobile any day! It's got a turbo-charged engine and three JUMBO exhaust pipes. And see these cannons? Well, they fire stuff too, so… pttttthhhhhhhhhhh!"

Shifty and Sam frowned. Surely cannons weren't allowed!

But Peregrine Pug was now waving his flag…

"On your marks – get set – GO!"

ZOOOOOM!

As Red Rocket blasted off, his exhaust pipes gushed out great clouds of smoke right in front of the Bakemobile's windscreen.

"Arggh!" cried the boys. They couldn't see a thing!

Shifty turned on the wipers full blast and headed through the smoke at a snail's pace. By the time they could see again the other racers

13

were miles ahead.

"Grrr!" grumbled Shifty. "We'll never catch them now."

"Course we will!" cried Sam.

They just needed to go faster. And Sam had just the thing…

Rummaging around in his cake-toppings tin, he whipped out a small glass jar. It was full of super-strength popping candy sprinkles.

Quickly, Sam opened a hatch into the engine and tapped in a few tiny sprinkles.

Shifty saw what he was doing. "That's not popping candy, is it? That's really powerful stuff!"

"Just a teeny bit. It'll make us go faster!" nodded Sam.

He didn't know for sure it would. But it had to be worth a try. They had to catch up with that silly Red Rocket before he tricked the other racers too!

Sam was just about to re-cork the jar when the van hit a pothole and –

WHOOSH!

ALL the popping candy (and the jar as well!) went tumbling into the engine.

"Ooops!" gasped Sam.

"What?" cried Shifty, his eyes still fixed on the road.

"Um, nothing!" squeaked Sam. "But you might just want to … hold tight!"

B4KE 1

17

For a wonderful moment nothing happened.

Then the van did a great smelly BURP – and leaped forward like a bucking bull!

Pots crashed down – bink! bonk! tshhhh!

Pans crashed down – kerr-doinnnnng!

And speeding forward, the van burped on…

Burp!

Vroooom!

Burrrp!

Vroooooom!

BUUUrrrP!!!

When they reached the corn maze the
Bakemobile burped its last burp. Then
thankfully, it seemed back to normal. But now
they had to find their way through the maze.

To be helpful, Sam switched on the tracking-
screen and called out clear directions.

"OK, Shifty – drive past the corn!"

"But it's ALL corn, Sam!"

"Oh yeah."

They drove around for what seemed like hours before the tracking-screen finally found the way out. The boys then followed a large race arrow that said: To Christmas Wood.

And this would have been a very good plan. Except the arrow did NOT lead to Christmas Wood, but to a big muddy BOG instead...

"Arggggggggh!" Shifty slammed on the brakes and the Bakemobile stopped just in time. The boys got out and couldn't believe their eyes. Stuck knee-deep in pongy mud were loads of their fellow racers!

"Really!" puffed Duchess, so covered in mud that she looked like a swamp monster.

"Whatever was Peregrine Pug thinking?"

"Fancy putting the sign the wrong way round!" scowled Hercules.

Shifty and Sam helped everyone out. Then they whisked them up mugs of hot chocolate in the back of the Bakemobile.

"But Sam," said Shifty, "it's not *like* Peregrine to get his signs muddled up."

"Unless," replied Sam, "SOMEBODY turned that sign round on purpose."

His eyes met Shifty's and they both gave a nod…

"Red Rocket!"

Leaving their friends drying out round a campfire, the boys set off for Christmas Wood. The more excited Red Rocket became, the more ridiculous his pranks became too. They needed to stop him before he went too far.

In no time at all, Shifty and Sam had found their way to Christmas Wood. As Shifty drove through it, Sam searched for tyre-tracks using his trusty BUN-oculars.

"There!" he pointed. They looked like the tracks Red Rocket's castle-tank would make. Shifty nodded. "Let's follow them – quick!"

The tracks wove in and out of the trees. Then into a tunnel-like cave. It was dark in the cave. But Shifty flicked a switch and the van's front bumper spun around to show a row of cream-horn shaped headlights. Each one was casting a beam as bright as a lighthouse!

They hurried along. And all was going well
until they were driving out of the cave. Then—
"Whoa!" cried Shifty. The van was slipping all
over the place!

With that, it whooshed out of the cave into
an even more slippery clearing.
Lots of other racers were
sliding round it too, like a
whirl of clumsy ice skaters!

FINISH
LINE!

MAT 15

FR4D

"Help!" called Rover.

Beep! Beep! Matilda tooted as everyone went swirling into the middle. Round and round – like water down a plughole, until…

CRASH!

ROV R

Chapter
Four

"Oil!" cried Shifty, examining the ground. "I bet that was Red Rocket again!"

"Grrr!" grumbled Sam. Their nincompoop neighbour never knew when to stop! But this time someone might have been hurt…

"Red Rocket mustn't win!" Matilda frowned.

"He's a cheat!" chorused all of her puppies.

"Stop him! Stop him! Stop him!" chanted the crowd.

Shifty nodded. "But how can we stop him?"

"The Bakemobile's wrecked," sighed Sam. "We couldn't even stop a flea in that!"

"Don't worry," piped up Rover. "I'll help you fix it up!"

"Us too!" cried everyone.

"Thanks guys!" the boys replied.

With everyone lending a helping paw, the Bakemobile was fixed in no time. Shifty started the engine. But, by now, Red Rocket would be miles ahead…

"Time to take to the sky!" Shifty nodded.

"You mean," Sam rubbed his paws together, "we can actually try out my NEVER-before-tested-but-very-probably-OK flying switch?!"

Shifty gave a little nod. "Sure can!"

Beaming, Sam flicked a switch on the dashboard and the cupcake on their roof gave a buzz.

From under it shot out three helicopter blades made from super-sized kitchen spatulas. But the question was … would the Bakemobile actually fly?

The spatulas started spinning around, slowly at first. But they soon picked up speed until they were going really fast.

Then the boys felt the van lift off the ground.

Up, up
and away!

"Oh boy!" cried Sam, now high above the treetops. "We're really flying!"

Shifty flew off over Christmas Wood and across to Rocky Road Mountain.

"There!" cried Sam.

He pointed at a tiny Red Rocket racing down the mountain below them to the finish line. Shifty swooped down and landed, transforming the Bakemobile back to normal to finish the race fair and square.

But wait! Red Rocket had heard them.

"Not you two losers!" he scowled. With that, all his cannons turned towards the Bakemobile, and—

BOOM!!!

A dozen gloopy custard pies hit the
Bakemobile's windscreen – splattttttttt!

Grabbing his Cupcake-Catapult, Sam loaded
it up with eclairs. If Red Rocket wanted a food
fight – he'd get one! Sam quickly took aim out
of the van's window and let ALL the eclairs
fly...

Whooosh!

They zoomed through the air and landed
perfectly in Red Rocket's cannons.

"You—!"
Red Rocket
stamped his little furry
foot. "You've BUNGED
UP my cannons, you meanies! I
am so telling on you! Grrrrrrrrr!!!"

In a full-on, fist-waving temper tantrum, Red Rocket spun off the track. Now the way to the finish line was clear for Shifty and Sam. But all of a sudden they heard a faint toot! toot!

It was Hercules
on his scooter!

FINISH
LINE!

ROVR

Shifty and
Sam knew how much
Hercules longed to win.
"Oh no!" called Shifty, suddenly
wiggling the steering wheel from side
to side like mad. "Something's wrong with
the Bakemobile! We're slowing down! We'll
NEVER win now!"

37

Shifty winked at Sam. And Sam winked back, happy to pretend the Bakemobile was broken if it meant that *Hercules* could win.

Tooting like mad, Hercules zoomed past them and flew across the finish line.

"Yay!" He punched the air with his tiny fist. "I DID it!"

To toast the new little champ, Shifty and Sam made everyone milkshakes.

They even made one for Red Rocket – who slurped it down – even though he said it tasted YUCK!

To Catch a Thief

Chapter One

"Shifty!" cried Sam. "Look at this! There's a robber in town!"

Sam banged his newspaper down so hard that his breakfast egg jumped out of its eggcup and landed in Shifty's lap.

"Careful!" gasped Shifty, and he quickly read the story.

Sam was right. A thief had been striking posh hotels around town and stealing from their richest guests.

An emerald necklace had been stolen from a world-famous opera singer. A gold watch had been swiped from a visiting president. And a pair of jewel-studded cufflinks, two ruby rings, and a whole box of piggy-shaped truffles (with raspberry centres) had been pinched from a millionaire chocolate-factory owner, who was on holiday with his family.

SPORT

THE CRIMES

Suddenly there was a knock at the door and
Lady Woofington burst in.

"Oh, boys – have you read about the thief?" she cried.

Lady W was in such a flap. Even her tiara was wonky! So Shifty and Sam sat her down with some tea and freshly baked croissants.

"The thing is," she spluttered, flecks of croissant flying everywhere, "my cousin, Lady Penelope Poshington, flew over from America yesterday. She's staying over at Toffworth Hall. And everyone knows that's the smartest hotel around!"

Lady Woofington swallowed her croissant and the boys leaned in a little closer.

"I'm certain," she said, "that the thief will try to rob Penny. Her jewellery is worth a fortune! How dreadful would it be – flying all the way here to have her prize diamonds pinched from right under her nose!"

Lady Woofington gulped down some tea. "So that's where *you* two can help!"

"Us?" said the boys.

"Of course!" cried Lady W. "You're super at catching thieves! You must go to Toffworth Hall at once and pretend that you work there. Then you must figure out who the thief is and catch them!"

This sounded very exciting. "Top plan!" cried Shifty, and Sam gave an eager nod.

They wolfed down their breakfast, grabbed some "catching-thieves" gadgets and emergency disguise accessories, and set off in the Bakemobile at once.

"We'll need to borrow some uniforms," said Sam, "to make it look like we work at the hotel."

"I bagsy being someone important," smiled Shifty. "Maybe head waiter or top chef!"

"Yeah," beamed Sam. "Or manager of the whole hotel!"

Chapter Two

As soon as they got to Toffworth Hall, Shifty
and Sam set about snaffling some uniforms.
But there was hardly anything to choose from
in the staff dressing room...

"A doorman!" groaned Shifty, plodding back
out in a suit that would fit a giant.

"Huh!" puffed Sam. "Don't YOU complain!
Look at me!"

They were just about to go and sniff out the
robber when up marched the hotel manager.

"Oi – you two!"

Mr Benson roared. "Stop hanging around like
wet shrimps!"

He read the name on Shifty's badge.

"Right, Henry!" he boomed. "Outside to lug luggage!" Then his eyes flicked to Sam's badge.

"And you, um, Edith – arrange these flowers in room twelve while Lady Poshington is downstairs having lunch."

He tossed a big bunch of flowers at Sam, then glared at Shifty again.

"Look smart then, Henry!" Mr Benson roared, following Shifty downstairs to where loads of luggage was piled up.

Sam headed off with the flowers. But then he had a brilliant idea! This was the perfect chance to use one of his new GADGETS.

While he was in Lady Poshington's room he'd slip an exploding cake box into her safe. Then the moment the thief went to grab her jewels – BOOM! The robber would be sticky-toffee-puddinged to the spot!

Sam had no trouble cracking the easy-peasy code Lady Poshington had chosen for her safe. He placed the exploding cake box inside, carefully re-locked the safe door, and finally shoved Lady Poshington's flowers into a vase.

Meanwhile, Shifty was out on the
drive when a shiny vintage car pulled
up. Its driver was a tall, smart otter in
a fine wool suit and silk cravat. As he
stepped out, Mr Benson welcomed
him and Shifty unloaded his suitcase.

"Now, Henry," Mr Benson said,
"kindly show Mr Otterby to
room thirteen."

The gentleman-otter followed Shifty inside and across the hall's marbled floor.

"Nice chandelier!" Mr Otterby smiled. "Top crystal."

They headed on, past the dining-room door. But Mr Otterby stopped at its entrance.

"And look at that diamond cluster necklace!" he exclaimed. "Who is that?"

He pointed at the elegant Afghan hound in a sparkly diamond necklace, sipping soup. Shifty guessed at once that this had to be Lady Woofington's cousin, Lady Poshington.

"Well, that's—" began Shifty. But Mr Otterby had swept in and was eyeing Lady Poshington's jewels.

"Hmm…" muttered Shifty. Could this otter be … the thief?!

Shifty bounded upstairs to report back to Sam, and met him backing out of Lady P's room.

"Shifty!" whispered Sam. "I've just booby-trapped the—"

"—Sam!" whispered Shifty at the very same time. "I've just sniffed out the robber! He's—"

But Shifty stopped. For who should he see skulking along the corridor but ... Mr Benson.

He seemed edgy and hot, and kept looking over his shoulder, like he was up to no good.

"Why's he creeping?" whispered Sam. "Wait – could *he* be the *robber*??"

"No!" Shifty whispered back. "The robber's an *otter*."

But even Shifty had to agree the hotel manager was looking mighty dodgy. What was he doing creeping about like a rat?!

"Argggh!" shrieked Mr Benson as he spotted the boys. He went as white as a sheet.

"I was j-just," he stuttered, swallowing hard. But taking a deep breath, he straightened up and was back to his grumpy old self.

"Right, Henry!" he snapped. "Get that suitcase into room thirteen while I … check Lady Poshington's safe – to make sure n-nothing's been stolen."

"Not the safe!" squeaked Sam. "You c-can't touch the safe!" But Mr Benson had already gone in.

"Why, Sam?" whispered Shifty. "Just what have you done?"

"I – nothing!" gulped Sam, stuffing his fingers in his ears, as…

Boom!

Chapter Three

Mr Benson made a very SOUR sticky-toffee-pudding.

Luckily for Sam, Mr Benson had no idea where the exploding cake box had come from. But unluckily for Sam, being a maid, he had to clean up the mess!

For the rest of the afternoon the boys were run off their feet, mopping, carrying suitcases, dusting, carrying suitcases, vacuuming, carrying suitcases. On, and on, and ON!

Then finally, just before afternoon tea was due to be served in the dining room, Henry and Edith were finally allowed a break.

"Here!" whispered Shifty, handing Sam some fake cupcakes with hidden cameras inside.

"We'll plant these Cam-Cupcakes on the cake stands in the dining room. That way we can keep a close eye on that scheming Mr Otter-thief!"

So, up in the dining room, while pretending to water the plants, Sam slyly planted the Cam-Cupcakes. Then he scuttled back to Shifty.

EDITH

"Mission accomplished!" he smiled.

Nodding, Shifty turned on a screen and the Cam-Cupcakes in the dining room bleeped on. Then tiny periscopes peeped up out of the fake icing.

"There he is!" Shifty cried as their suspect sipped his tea. The otter's eyes, they saw, were fixed firmly on Lady Poshington.

"They're getting on really well!" snorted Sam. "I think he wants to be … her boyfriend!"

"Pffffff!" Shifty wrinkled up his nose and sniggered. "Ewwwww!"

But the boys soon had the smiles wiped off their faces when Mr Otterby picked up a Cam-Cupcake and popped it into his MOUTH!

"He's eating our camera!" spluttered Sam as their screen went dark and fuzzy. A moment later, the screen flashed on again. But now they could only see bits of cherry and clumps of soggy cake floating past…

"That's – that's – stuff in his tummy!" Shifty shuddered. "YUCK!"

Change of plan. They would have to track the robber with their own eyes! But when they reached the dining room…

"Uh-oh!"

The robber's chair was BARE!

"I bet," whispered Sam, "he's gone to pinch the jewels out of Lady P's safe!"

"Right then," Shifty nodded back. "After him!"

Chapter Four

"He's not here!" panted Shifty, bursting into Lady Poshington's room. They checked her safe. It was still full of jewels.

With that, the boys heard footsteps outside. Mr Otterby was coming...

"Hide!"

They dived under the bed and waited as the thief crept in. As he crossed the room, Shifty and Sam could only see his feet.

"Wait till he gets the jewels," whispered
Shifty. "Then, when he's sneaking back out, I'll
grab him round the ankle."

Sam gave a little nod. "Genius!"

They heard the safe's dial whirr and click.
Then the clink of jewellery being bundled into
a bag.

Next, they heard the safe door close and the
sound of footsteps again.

"He's coming," whispered Sam, and Shifty
nodded.

"I'm ready…"

They waited until the robber's feet came
into view, then Shifty shot out a nifty paw and
grabbed him round the ankle.

"Argggggh!" The robber started to tumble.
"Help!"

As he fell, the thief grabbed at the bedclothes, trying to steady himself. But instead he just pulled the quilt down with him and landed in a heap – with the quilt over his head…

"Nooooo!"

Shifty and Sam flew from under the bed and dived on top of the quilt. Under it Mr Otterby was trying to wriggle out.

"Oh, no you don't!" Shifty cried.

With that, the bedroom door opened and in stepped Lady Poshington. "Goodness!" she gasped.

"Don't worry – your jewels are fine!" panted Sam.

"Because *we* caught the thief!" Shifty added. He pointed to the quilt. "He's under here – it's Mr Otterby!"

But Shifty had barely finished speaking when who should he notice in the corridor but ... Mr Otterby!

75

"Eh?" Shifty gaped.

"Wha—" gulped Sam. How could the thief be out *there*, when he was *here* – trapped under this quilt?

Unless Mr Otterby was NOT the thief after all…?

"I'm a policeman!" the otter announced, stepping in through the door. "PC Holt at your service! I've been working undercover, keeping an eye on the suspect! Ah, but I see you've captured him *for* me – thank you!"

With that, PC Holt grabbed the quilt and whisked it off the real thief.

"You!" cried Shifty, and Sam's eyes grew wide...

EDITH

"MR BENSON!"

The master jewel-thief narrowed his eyes. "You meddling hounds!" he roared. "I nearly got away with it too! Grrrrrrr!"

PC Holt told everyone that Mr Benson's *real* name was Benny Lightpaw. He said that the police had been after him for ages, but he'd been very good at disguising himself as he'd found job after job at the fanciest hotels in town.

As PC Holt carted Benny off, Lady Poshington looked like she might faint from shock.

"This calls for some strong, sweet tea!" said Shifty, whisking her back to the lounge. Sam thought some "strong, sweet cakes" would be good for her too!

"Let's take a photo to show Lady Woofington that your jewels are safe," said Sam. "We'll use a Cam-Cupcake."

"Say cheese!" Shifty grinned.

"No way," giggled Sam. "Say posh doughnut!"

The Mystery Parcel

"Bye, Scottie," said Shifty.

"Bye, Scottie," said Sam. "Hope you'll feel better soon!"

Scottie dabbed his runny red nose. "Tanks, boys."

Poor Scottie had been under the weather all week. So Shifty and Sam had baked him a cake to cheer him up.

Scottie loved cake and the boys had loved

making it! There was nothing better than baking with your best friend, after all.

They'd agreed, after watching a movie about knights and dragons with Scottie a few days ago, that his "Get Well!" cake would be a super-cool dragon.

Leaving the cake on Scottie's bedside table, the boys hurried outside. It was raining, but they had to get back to their café quickly to open up for the day.

84

Jumping on
their bikes, they set off at
once, splashing through the puddles. And
as they got to the café door they saw that the
postman had been...

"Oh!" said Shifty.

"Oh!" said Sam.

"A parcel!"

As Sam wheeled the bikes in from the rain,
Shifty carried in the parcel. But no sooner had
he popped it down, than Sam was beside him,
his ears pricked up and his eyes wide with
excitement.

This parcel was a mystery!

Who had sent it?

And who was it for?

"It's clearly for me – see there!" beamed
Sam, trying to read the rain-smudged label.

"That plippy-ploppy smudge CLEARLY
looks like an 'S'. And that splurty-wurty wiggle
is an 'm'!"

Shifty shook his head. He didn't want to fall
out. But Sam was clearly mistaken.

"No," said Shifty. "All those squiggles spell 'Shifty'. There are too many for it to say 'Sam'. Sam only has three letters: S-a-m, whereas Shifty has LOTS of letters, see?"

Sam opened his mouth but Shifty went on, "Besides, I'm not being rude, Sam, but … I'm actually *taller* than you!"

Sam gaped. That had nothing to do with anything!

"Well, I'm not being rude either," Sam frowned. "But at least *I* don't look like … a giraffe!"

Shifty dived on the box.

"Mine!" he cried.

Sam dived on the box.

"No, mine!"

And the rest of the morning went something like this…

"Mine, Giraffe-neck!"

"Mine, Doughnut-tum!"

"Are you saying I'm fat?"

"Are you saying I'm neck-y?"

"Mine!"
"Mine!"
"Oi!"
"GET OFF!"

Chapter
Two

The café didn't open that morning. It opened
in the afternoon. And when it did, it looked a
little different…

"What's this?" said Rover, stepping through
the door, a stream of customers behind him.
Dividing the café exactly in two was a waist-
high wall of cake boxes.

"We are now TWO cafés!" Shifty announced.
"Because – see that parcel there?

Well, it's MINE."

With that, Sam's head popped over the wall.

"It isn't!

It's MINE!"

Sam looked at the gaping customers at the door.

"Anyway, guys – come to *my* side," he called. "'Cos I'm giving out free cookies!"

"You c-can't do that!" Shifty spluttered.

"Can too!" snorted Sam.

Shifty thought for a moment. "Well, then!" he said. "I'm giving out free EVERYTHING!"

"Yay!" A stream of customers raced to his side. "Free EVERYTHING!"

But suddenly Rover raised a paw. "Stop right there!" he cried. The customers stopped and their faces fell.

"Doh!" tutted Dotty. Free EVERYTHING looked to be off the menu!

"Guys, why not *open* the parcel?" suggested Rover. "That might help you decide who it's for."

Shifty nodded. Sam nodded too. So Rover opened it and the boys peered in...

"WOW!"

In the box was the most amazing dragon costume the boys had EVER seen. It was green and scaly, with flappy wings – and a long pointy tail!

Shifty had not ordered this costume. Nor had Sam. So how could they decide (in a grown-up way) who should have it?

Shifty thought.

Sam did too.

"I challenge you to a joust on horseback!" cried Sam. "Like the knights did in that film we saw."

"I accept your challenge!" Shifty nodded, standing tall.

"Whoa!" cried Rover. "Knights? Horses? Somebody might get hurt!"

But Shifty and Sam had decided. A joust it would be!

Rover told the boys there had to be rules.

"Firstly, you must ride on your *bikes*," he said. "Because horses are far too dangerous." He pointed to their bikes, now dry, over in the corner.

"Secondly," said Rover, "you must dress up like knights. And finally – no prodding each other with your lances. You must prod *cakes* off cake stands instead. The one who knocks off the most cakes will win Duchess's hand in marriage!"

"I think not!" cried Duchess.

"The dragon costume!" shouted Sam.

"Sorry! Yes! The dragon costume." Rover blushed.

The boys began to get everything ready to joust.

"Right," cried Sam, legging it to the stock cupboard. "I bagsy the tinfoil for my armour!"

"No way!" roared Shifty. "That tinfoil is definitely MINE!"

Chapter Three

The park was all set for the big joust when
Sam squeaked up on his "horse".

"I, Sir Ever-so-Tall," he cried, "am ready to
joust to the END!"

"Oooh!" gasped Hercules, clapping his paws.
"Wicked!"

All the café customers were dressed up too,
cartons of popcorn at the ready. And over on
the bank, in pride of place, was the

dragon costume.

Sam raised his lance. (It was really a baguette, but it did the job rather well.)

"But where is my dastardly opponent?!" he frowned.

With that, in pedalled Shifty – freshly baked lance at the ready.

"I, Sir Taller-than-YOU, am here – to take up the challenge!" he cried.

"Then let the battle commence!" announced Rover.

Sir Peregrine-of-Pugland put his trumpet to his lips. "Pa pa pa pa pa pa paaa!"

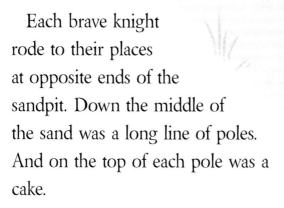

Each brave knight
rode to their places
at opposite ends of the
sandpit. Down the middle of
the sand was a long line of poles.
And on the top of each pole was a
cake.

The winner of the splendid dragon costume
would be the knight who knocked the most
cakes down.

Rover raised his flag. "Get set... CHARGE!"
And Shifty and Sam were off!

The crowd started screaming and roaring
their names...

"Sir Ever-so-Tall!"
"Sir Taller-than-YOU! Woo hoo!"

Donk!
Donk!
Donk!

Sir Ever-so-Tall was doing well as cakes tumbled left, right and centre! But Sir Taller-than-YOU was doing even better.

"I'm going to win!" Shifty called, as they turned for the final round.

"Oh, no you're not!" shouted Sam. "NO WAY!"

But Sam knew he would have to do better if he was going to win this tournament. Sir Taller-than-YOU was only winning because he was so jolly tall!

"Right," muttered Sam under his breath. It was time to get clever!

Earlier, when decorating his bike, Sam had also fitted a cunning gadget to jack up his seat and make *him* the tallest knight in the kingdom! And now was the time to see if it actually worked...

With his lance, Sam secretly jabbed a button just behind his horse's ear.

ZOOP! His seat went up, but just a little bit.

Shifty saw. "Hey!" he frowned.

But Sam still wasn't tall enough so he pressed the button again. And this time Sam kept his lance pressed firmly down...

With a wheezy whirr and a noisy clunk – *ZOOP!* – Sam's seat shot up so fast he was flung high into the air.

"Argghh!" Sam wailed as he zoomed like a firework.

"Help!"

Chapter
Four

SPLASH!

Sam landed in the duck pond and
disappeared under the water.

"Sam!" yelled Shifty, racing over and diving
in after him.

Everyone followed, only to see Shifty
disappear underwater too! A few seconds later
there was a ripple of bubbles…

BLOOP!
BLOOP!
BLOOP!

Then up from the water Shifty popped –
holding a very soggy Sam.

"Here!" called Rover, reaching out a
baguette. "Shifty! Grab hold of this!"

Shifty grabbed it and Rover swiftly pulled
them from the water.

As Sam dripped on the bank
looking glum, Shifty went off
for the costume.

"Here, Sam …
you can have it,"
he said kindly.

He'd much rather have his best friend back than a dragon costume any day. Quarrelling with Sam had been the worst thing ever!

"No," Sam managed a little smile. "You should have it, Shifty. You did rescue me after all."

"Or maybe you could *share* it?" suggested Rover. "Take turns to wear it, eh?"

"Good plan!" said Shifty, and Sam gave a nod.

"Perfect!"

Now that was decided, it was time for a picnic. Shame to waste all those knocked-down cakes!

The friends gathered them up and blew off the sand. Then everyone sat on picnic blankets, tucking in!

They had only just finished when...

119

"Boys!" came a voice, and up pattered Scottie, looking much better.

"I just called round to the café," he said. "But there was nobody there. Then I bumped into Fred who said you were here."

"Yes," said Sam. "We've been... Well, it doesn't matter!"

"Anyway," smiled Scottie, "I called round to pick up my new costume."

"*Your* costume?!" gasped Shifty.

"This dragon one?" gasped Sam.

"Sure!"

When Scottie had watched that knight movie with Shifty and Sam, he had liked the dragon best.

"I ordered my costume right after that!" Scottie said with a grin. "And it looks just like that awesome dragon cake you baked me."

"I LOVE it!"

He explained that he'd left instructions for the costume to be delivered to the café, in case he was too poorly to get out of bed.

"Was that OK?" he said to the boys. "I hope it didn't cause any bother?"

"Bother?" giggled Shifty.

"Bother!" giggled Sam. "Not a bit!"

Scottie popped on the costume. "And now," he said, "let's all play Dragon CHASE!"

"Yay! Good idea!" everyone cried.
And for *once*...

...the knights let the dragon do the chasing!

"Rahhhhhhhh!"